THE DROID

MAYANK SINHA

BlueRose ONE.com
Stories Matter

First Published in March 2023

ISBN: 978-93-5741-138-7

BLUEROSE PUBLISHERS

www.BlueRoseONE.com

info@bluerosepublishers.com

+91 8882 898 898

Cover Design:

Tyngshain Pariat

Typographic Design:

Rohit

Distributed by: BlueRose, Amazon, Flipkart

Dedicated

To all my mentors who always had faith in me.

CONTENTS

The Blue Light 1

The Orb 10

Dreams 17

The Mine 19

The Lab 24

The Portal 34

A New World 38

Ten years 46

The Programmers 49

The Beginning 54

THE
BLUE LIGHT

Those times must have been great when humans weren't immortal. I guess life would've been a lot different than it is now. It all started almost a hundred years ago, in the 21st century, when the human race was quickly advancing in the field of technology. A scientist named James Corning made a breakthrough in neural networking. He was able to use his mind as a processing machine to scavenge data from the internet. He created a chip that we call the Neural Bridge Linking Chip or NBLC for short. This chip was a quantum computing microprocessor that could interface itself with the human brain and act as an over-guiding CPU. This chip was also able to use the brain's capabilities in data processing and storage to perform tasks that once seemed impossible.

The company marketed the NBLC as a tool to enhance the capabilities of the human brain. Initially, it was said that the person using it had access to all the information in the world as the NBLC had an interface to connect to the internet. Information was only a thought away. It seemed as if the human brain now had no limits to what it could achieve. This seemed to be true for some time as well. Lead scientists and researchers were the first to use the chip. A landslide of breakthroughs started happening. In a matter of years, cancer was cured. Every fatal disease seemed to have become as simple as the common cold. Epileptic attacks became a thing of the past. A golden age of the human race had begun.

But good things seldom last. As the chip became public, people began to use it for various crimes and hacks as well. The government had to pass several new laws to keep the crimes in check. Corning industries then launched ASM, an AI which came embedded in the chip to prevent its misuse.

Now that I look back, I think there is a reason that the rich remained rich, because even with the enhanced potential of the chip, the people were still not able to handle their success. In the golden age, many people made millions through their ideas and businesses, but within a year, they were unable to handle their wealth and faced the problem of having too much money. Despite having earned so much, they lost everything and the final result was a recession that had never happened before.

That recession changed everything, from economic policies to the way money is handled. It was in those times that the people recognized the human body as a liability. First, different genetic enhancements were tried to create a breed of superhumans who could survive in extreme weather and temperature conditions. But still, the need for food to run the body, even though in a small quantity, and the ageing process of the body remained a major liability.

This is where the NBLC chip did what nobody had imagined in their wildest dreams. With the help of neural mapping and using the NBLC as a base, a team at Corning industries was successfully able to convert the human consciousness into data. And as a result, they were able to copy and transfer it into another host, which we call as AMDs (All Metal Droids). Once this was done, the human body lost its value. It seems that consciousness was the only thing that kept humans attached to the flesh. And once it was possible to transfer it, there was no need to keep the flesh body alive to handle its slow degradation over time. And the human race, in theory, became immortal, detached from the strings of time.

Today, the economy seems to have stabilized. The government partnered with Corning industries to overlook and maintain the usage of the NBLC. Now anyone above the age of twenty-five can opt for becoming a droid. The only clause that comes with it is that when opting to be a droid, you have to sign a contract to serve Corning industries in one way or the other and any new achievement or invention made while the chip is planted automatically becomes a proprietary of Corning industries. There are some exclusions to the age limit law, such as any terminally ill person can opt for the transfer even before the age of twenty-five by the legal consent of their guardians. This brings us to me.

My name is Max. I became a droid when I was around a year old. I had bone marrow cancer since birth and becoming a droid was the only way I could survive. I am what they call a virtual orphan. I never knew my parents as the orphanage where I grew up said that one night, somebody left me at their doorstep wrapped in a white cloth and only with a small note that read 225-456-998-764-598, at the bottom. It was signed by Jade. I guess this is my mother's name. I tried to find her as I grew up by using these numbers, but I never traced anything about her. By human years I'll be turning twenty-one this month. I work as a hardware engineer at a droid manufacturing factory of Corning industries. As a droid, I can enjoy human food as well. My taste and smell sensors help me in it. Being a droid is fun stuff, except for the fact that I have to always try not to run completely out of power. The droids look the same as humans, but their internal frame is made up of titanium. My job is to ensure that all the hardware installed in the droid is ready to interface with the NBLC chip and also do a dry run of the droid before it is sent out to a customer. My job is not an exciting one, but it still has some moments of fun in it. Like one time, when I was trying to do a dry run of the droid, it seemed that due to a defect, the interface of hands and legs got interchanged, and so when I switched it on for testing, it immediately stood on its arms and I had to call for help to catch this gymnastic handstand droid. It was both hilarious and scary to see this droid try to eat a banana by his feet.

I have a decent life. I work for ten hours on weekdays and then on weekends, I do volunteer work at the orphanage where I was brought up. It's good to see the children learning to speak and walk. It fills me with delight. I am very much fascinated by the NBLC's functioning in children. Even though it is embedded in the child, it is still preferred that the child is taught everything from scratch like a human instead of just uploading every skill into the chip itself. I guess the reason behind it is to preserve the human part of the psyche of the child. We droids also have a bed to sleep on, just like our human counterparts. The only difference is that our B.E.D stands for Battery Enabled Dock, and it also serves as our charging station.

One day, I was walking toward my home after my shift was over. It had gotten late, so no means of transport was available. Even though I am a droid, I still prefer to travel by a vehicle whenever possible because it prevents my motors from overheating and increases their lifespan. But to be honest, I am a little lazy.

The walk from my office to my flat takes about thirty minutes. As I was walking down the street, it seemed like a normal night. The street lights in front of me painted the area with a yellowish hue. The road was empty, and on the far end of the street, I could see a homeless guy (or droid) trying to start a fire in an empty 20Ltr oil can. There was no sound except for the random sound from the guy's rants and the 'CLANK' sound as he dropped things in the empty tank. I did not want any unnecessary conflict, so I just kept walking straight, ignoring the guy.

Homeless guy: "Aye! Yo! Buddy! Where are you going?"
I ignored it.
Homeless guy: "Oyii! Hello! I am talking to you."
I ignored again and quickened my pace.
Homeless guy: "Aye! Man! Don't you run! Are you a pussy now?"

Even though I am a droid, I am still a man. I know that the smallest unit of life is an atom, which consists of electrons, protons, and neutrons. And if you split an electron into a hundred parts, you will get the size of the male ego. And being called a pussy by another man had hurt it, so I stopped. I looked at the guy and yelled, "No!!! Your mother must be lonely. That's why I have to hurry man!!"

Homeless guy: "Oh!! Shit!! Ahaaaa! My Man! Come over here man, have a drink with me. Here, I've got beer".

"Okay, Fuck it." I whispered to myself and started walking toward the guy.

He handed me a beer bottle, and we did cheers.

Homeless guy: "So, I am Sam. What's your name?"

Me: "I am Max."

By his looks and his fidgety hands, I figured that he was a human.

Sam: "So, where were you going?"

Me: "I was just heading home."

Sam: "Ah! Okay. You see, man, this here (pointing to the street) is my home. I was born and raised here. And I hope to die here as well. "

Me: "Oh, okay."

Sam: "See man, I never had any family to look up to or connect to. I've lived like a lone wolf until now. You do the same, my man. These bitches are just crazy! They only want your money and shit."

Me: "Hmm. Okay! I'll keep that in mind. So, what are you doing here?"

Sam: "Oh, nothing much, just got these scraps from the wood chipper to be burned off. That's all. I work at this wood factory as a carpenter. "

Me: "Oh! So you're not homeless?"

Sam: "Homeless? What shit nigga? The beer getting you already Han!!"

Me: "Oh no, I… I am sorry. I… just thought you were…"

Sam: "It's okay man. No harm, no foul. You know, I've been here for almost thirty years. I started as a young guy just like you. And then…"

He continued speaking, but I couldn't pay attention to what he was saying.

HMMMM!!!! HMMM!!! HMMMM!! HMMMM!! HMMMMM!! This sound just started out of nowhere and was bothering me. My ears are more sensitive than the humans, so I figured why the guy was unaffected. This sound seemed to be coming from a distance, but was gradually coming closer.

Sam: ".....And then you know, my boss was like... what... how did you do.... Ah... I am gonna cherish this for my life. What the fuc......"

He started to frantically look around.

Sam: "Hey man. Do you hear that? What the fuck is that?"

Me: "Yeah, man. I can. I am not sure either."

HMMMMMMM!!! HMMMMMMM!!! HMMMMMM!!! HMMMMM!!

The sound was growing louder and was moving closer. In a matter of seconds, I could see a white strip stretched across the night sky. From the strip, a translucent blue light was appeared to be scanning the ground. Every time it hit the ground, a loud sound was heard.

I looked at Sam. Both of us didn't know what was happening, but we didn't want to be a part of it, so we threw our beer and made a run for it, away from the blue light. I could quickly feel the wind gushing as I was gaining speed.

THUD!! "Wait for me man!"

I looked back. Sam had fallen on the ground. I had forgotten that he was human and couldn't run that fast. I decided to go back to him. The blue light was inching closer to him. I was running as fast as I could to reach him in time. He was hurriedly trying to crawl away from the light. As soon as I reached him, I held his hand to pull him.

HMMMM!!! HMMMMM!!

Poof!!!

His whole body had turned to ash. I just stood there for a second, shocked at what I had just seen.

HMMMM!!

The sound brought me to my senses again, and I realized that the blue light was just inches away from me. I turned around to make a run for it. Clink! I turned to see the blue light touch the tip of my shoe's heel, but I didn't think much. I just started to run.

The first few steps seemed fine.

"ERROR 5901: Critical motor error. Left toe motor not responding" flashed before my eyes. I ignored it and tried to limp away from the light.

HMMM!!! HMMM!! HMM!!! The sound was now deafening me. I was limping as fast as I could.

"ERROR 6890: Critical motor error. Left knee motor not responding" flashed before my eyes. "Oh! Shit, shit!! Shit!! Before I could move, I fell to the ground. I was now trying to crawl away.

HMMMM! The light was now scanning my body. I knew it was too late.

"ERROR 6001: Critical joint error: Left hip joint not responding."

"ERROR 2001: Critical motor error. Right arm not responding"

"ERROR 4002: Critical motor error. Neck motor not responding"

"Major systems offline!. Initiating shutdown. Beacon activated." was the last thing that flashed before my eyes before everything went dark.

THE ORB

"System Boot up sequence initiated"

"Initializing systems…"

And slowly, everything started to come into focus. It took a second for my eyes to focus on the light that was shining on my face. It seemed like the light dentists use to look into the mouth. I realized I was in a droid repair facility, lying on a metal bench beneath the light. I slowly tried to sit up. I saw that my skin covering had been taken off and my titanium shell was visible.

"Oh, so you're awake," a voice came from behind. I turned to find an old man wearing a worker's apron and a green cap with a torch on it. He had a sandwich in one hand and a beer in his other, metal hand.

"So, how are you feeling?" he asked.

Me: "I feel Ok. My system checks are showing fine. But there is some dizziness in my optical sensors and my calibration of stance seems a little off. Ah… Who are you?"

"Oh, sorry! I forgot to introduce myself. I am Andrew Young. I am the repairman you were assigned to." he replied.

"And yeah, the dizziness is normal and just a sec, I'll check on your calibration." he added.

Me: "How did I get here?"

Andrew: "My team picked a distress beacon signal and it led us to you. We found you out cold on the street. Your whole neural circuit was fried. What the hell happened with you over there?"

Me: "I... I am not sure... I cannot remember clearly. I remember being there but… Ah, can you check my video logs of that night?"

Andrew: "I already did. The last log shows you leaving the factory. That's all. After that, it's a blank slate. Do you remember anything else from that night?"

Me: "Ah. I… I… think there was someone else with me."

"ERROR 1890: Memory block inaccessible. Memory might be corrupt" flashed before my eyes. "Ah!! Shit!"

Andrew: "What? What happened?"

Me: "Oh, it's nothing. My memory is inaccessible."

Andrew: "Oh, okay. Don't stress about it. I have replaced your neural network. It'll take some time for you to adjust to it. Let me run some basic diagnostics and then you will be good to go."

Me: "Okay. And thanks for the help."

Andrew: "No Problem buddy. Just take care and don't overload your circuits from now on."

Me: "Hmm. Okay."

I wore my skin and my clothes. And then I headed for my flat. It was becoming difficult for me to remember what had happened that night. My memory block was still inaccessible. So I decided not to stress on it much and wait for the memory block to be accessible again.

After reaching home, I saw that my battery was at 10%. I lay down on my bed. It was my day off. Only a few minutes had passed when I saw:

"Initiating nap sequence. Systems going on standby…" And everything became dark.

In the complete darkness, I could hear a faint voice. I decided to follow it. It was slowly becoming clearer.

"Aye man, don't leave me here…" I couldn't make out what it was.

HMMMMMMMMMM!!!!!!! A deafening sound came.

I woke up with a start. My core temperature had risen significantly. It took me a few seconds to come to my senses. And then I had to manually initiate the body cool down sequence. I was still not sure as to what had happened to me.

I looked at the clock. It was 6:00 AM. It was almost close to my time of waking up. I just thought to clear my head and get ready to go to work.

The memory error was not going away. It had now started to bother me. In my office, I had a spare droid diagnostics kit. I then decided to take matters into my own hands. During lunch hour, when most of the working platform became vacant, I hooked myself to the system. On trying to manually find the video log of that night, I came across a weird thing. The memory slots where the logs files would have been was missing a file. The last log was of my leaving the factory, but after that, there were no files. And the rest of the files resumed when I woke up in the repair facility.

Something seemed off to me as this had never happened before. And above all, it didn't make sense, because if Andrew was to be believed, then my neural network frying up due to an overload could have corrupted my memory log. But even in that case, the files would still have been there, instead of just an empty directory. I was not able to wrap my head around the incidents of that night. I suspected that while I was passed out, somebody manually started the sequence of a memory wipe. And when I tried to access it after waking up, I got the error that the file was inaccessible because at that time, the wipe-out procedure had locked the file. This came as a hunch as there was no other way to wipe a droid's memory without activating the droid first. But who? Or rather, why would anyone do that to me? It made no sense. I tried to find a logical explanation for all this and even tried to find an alternate theory, but any other option seemed impractical to me.

The empty memory slot was now bothering me and I wanted to find the truth behind it. I then returned to my workstation and continued with my work. Halfway through it, I heard a female's voice, "Max, is that you?" I looked up to see who was calling. But to my surprise, the other workstations were still empty. "Hey, don't you know me?", the voice came again. I looked around again and started scanning the area. But still, I got no results.

"Aye… Are you a pussy now?" I heard a different voice this time. I stood up and started to take a walk around the platform. Still, no one was nearby. I then checked my auditory sensors but they had not picked up any sounds either. It seemed that the voice was only in my head. This was a new experience for me as this had never happened before. This felt unreal to me.

"Are you there? Hehe…" the female voice questioned.

"Yes, I am" I replied. "Who are you?" I added.

"Max, is that you?" the voice asked again.

"Yes it's me! Who are you?"

"Hey, don't you know me?" After a few tries, I figured that only these three phrases were being repeated. I stopped replying and then the voices suddenly stopped.

While travelling home that night, my mind was occupied by these strange incidents. As the bus halted on a signal, something caught my eye. At a distance, I could see a white, brightly lit orb revolving around the lamp of a street light. It made me curious and unconsciously, I started to stare at it. After a few moments, the orb seemed to have caught my gaze and was now flying toward me. But before it could get to me, the bus started to move and the orb couldn't keep up. I tried to look through the window. But the bus's speed was too much. I then sat on my seat with a sigh. But suddenly, to my surprise, the orb was now floating by my side. The other passengers seemed oblivious to it. I tried to catch the orb, but my hand went right through it. I figured it was some kind of hologram. The orb seemed to have a mind of its own. It kept flowing all over the bus, as if looking for something. As I got down at my stop, it came with me, floating by my side. It seemed kind of cute, like a small child revolving around me as I walked home. I figured that it must be some sort of message hologram as these things are only visible to the concerned person and do not vanish until the message is received by the recipient.

As I sat down in my dining chair, the orb floated and rested on my lap. When I tried to touch it, it turned blue and a message popped up, followed by the voice note. "Hello, I am Kim, Kindly speak the username to proceed. "

"Max," I said.

Kim: "Wrong username. Please try again."

Me: "Ah... Maxwell."

Kim: "Wrong username. Please try again."

Me: "Ah... Max1234."

Kim: "Wrong username. Please try again."

Me: "Okay... Maxwell, all CAPS."

Kim: "Wrong username. Please try again."

Me: "Max, all CAPS."

Kim: "Wrong username. Please try again."

I was getting nowhere with this. It felt as if I was looking for a needle in a haystack. This orb came out of nowhere and was not providing me with any context as to where to start from.

TRING!! TRING!!! TRING!! TRING!! I was getting a call from an unknown number.

The orb floated away.

"Hello..." I said.

Operator: "Hello sir, this is a query call from the Droid police force regarding your recent repair. Is it a good time to talk?"

Me: "Yes, It's fine. How can I help you?"

Operator: "You are Mr. Maxwell, correct?"

Me: "Yes."

Operator: "You have recently come from a repair facility, correct?"

Me: "Yes."

Operator: "Okay. Were you sent to the repair facility due to an injury?"

Me: "Ah. Actually no… not that I can recall. Currently, my memory block is inaccessible."

Operator: "Oh, okay. No issues. You can reach us on the same number if you would like to report anything else. We will help you out. And one more thing, just for our records, are there any family or friends of yours that we can reach out to?"

Me: "No, sorry, I am an orphan. You can reach out to my orphanage where I was brought up. I will send you the details shortly."

Operator: "Oh, okay. Thank you for your time. Have a nice day."

The orb was still floating in one corner of the room, as if waiting for instructions.

I did not know how to handle it. So I let it be and headed for my bed as I had an early shift the next day.

My systems shut down rather quickly. I didn't get any shutdown message and was instantly surrounded by darkness.

DREAMS

I could hear footsteps. I could hear someone's rapid breathing. I tried to focus on the sound. And slowly, I could see. It was dusk time. There were many trees around, in every direction that I could see. The trees were tall and thick, it looked like I was in a forest. I was running frantically. I was panting for breath. My doctor's coat had become all muddy. A man wearing the same coat was in front of me, and a woman was behind us. It seemed as if we were trying to run away from something.

The woman held my hand as we ran through the forest. I could see fear in her eyes as she looked at me. She held my hand tight. Just then, a white strip of light lit the sky behind us. And HMMMM!!!! echoed through the forest. I could see the blue light screen scanning the forest from a distance. The other man was not visible now. It was only the two of us, sweating, our hearts pounding, running out of breath, racing against the blue light, running with all we had as the sound with the light was coming closer.

Crack!! Thud!! The woman slipped and fell. And by the looks of it, she had sprained her ankle. I got her by the shoulder and was trying to get her through the forest as quickly as possible. My heart was beating against my chest. My lungs were ready to explode and my throat was parched. Still, I was not ready to give up.

HMMMM!!!! The light was getting closer. "Max, I don't think we are going to make it." the woman said, barely able to breathe. I was exhausted too. I looked her in the eye. We both knew it was true. "Here, take the capsule and go. Leave me or both of us will die."

"No, never! Are you crazy? I am not leaving you here!" I finally managed to speak.

"Max, just take the capsule and leave." the woman said.

The blue light had almost caught up with us. "No, I am not leaving you here. If I am going to die here, I am going to die with you." I said. The woman smiled. There were tears in her eyes. We hugged tightly. The blinding light and the deafening sound engulfed us.

"Jade….." I whispered. I woke up with a start. I looked around. My core had heated up again. It took me a while to come to my senses. My sensor readings were normal. But my neural activity was off the charts. I sat on my bed after initiating the manual cooldown.

Just then, from the corner of the room, I heard. "Username Jade accepted." and the orb's color changed from blue to green. As I turned around to have a look, the orb floated toward me. I tried to touch it, and as it came in contact with my hand, it popped open and revealed a location coordinate. Then it disappeared into the air.

I entered the coordinates into my GPS and found out that it was the location of an iron ore mine hundred miles south from where I lived. My memory slot was still empty and I thought I needed a break. So I packed my things and decided to leave for the place. I still had no clue what I was doing, but it felt right.

The Mine

By public transit, it took me about two hours to reach the place. It was a small town named Hermshire. As I reached the town, it felt as if the town had this grey tinge to it. The town folk seemed quiet and preferred to mind their own business. I tried to talk with a few of them to query about the mine and how to get there, but they walked past me as if I didn't exist.

After a few more failures, I decided to find my way. After searching and walking around the town for almost an hour, I was finally able to find the sheriff's office. The office looked like a poor replica of the Texan style bar where the bad guys went for a drink and fistfights were only a beer can away.

As I walked into the office, the creaks in the wooden floor welcomed me. In front of me lied an empty desk and a chair. No one seemed to be around.

"Hello?. Is anyone there?" I asked.

I got no response.

"Hellooo…??" I repeated.

"Yeah!! In here mate…" someone replied.

I followed the voice and arrived in front of a back office. A plump old man in a police uniform and a cowboy hat sat behind a desk. He was eating what looked like a cheese hamburger and wiped his mouth with a handkerchief after every bite, but he was still not able to wipe the yellow tinge that the mustard sauce left on his bushy moustache. As I stood there, he suddenly looked up and with his half-filled mouth, said, "Hey mate. Have a seat. I will be with you in a minute".

I didn't want to interfere during his lunch time, so I sat quietly on a chair in the corner.

After finishing his delicacy, he wiped his mouth and went to wash his face. On returning, his belly bounced with each step. He then sat on his chair and signaled me to sit in front of him.

"Hello, son, I am Sheriff John tailor of Hermshire. How can I help you?" he asked.

"Hi, I am Max. I am here to visit the iron ore mine." "Visit? What is there to visit, son? The mine had closed years ago. And what would a young lad like you do in a mine?"

"Ah. I... I am a mine explorer. I like to explore old mines and make videos on them." I replied.

"Mine explorer? Never heard of that job before. But well, you kids these days are just doing things we old folk won't get. Ain't it, son?" he said and chuckled a bit.

I smiled hesitatingly.

"Don't worry, son. The entrance of the mine is two miles west to the town, in the woods. You can rent a bike from Peter's garage to get there and they will also toss in a map to the place. Just tell them, sheriff John sent ya. The garage is located on the third left of this place. But try to be back before the dark, kid, and try to not get into any trouble." he smiled and replied.

I smiled back and then headed to Peter's garage. Mr. Peter seemed like a nice man in his sixties. He was tall and smelled like grease and sweat. My conversation with him was brief yet good as he didn't try to take me to a walk down the memory lane. Instead, he just asked me where I wanted to go. He took some money as a security deposit for the bike and then handed me the bike keys and a walkie-talkie, in case I get stuck somewhere. And then I was on my way toward the mine.

It sometimes feels strange that we get so used to our daily life that we forget that this entire world exists right in front of us. We start living in this bubble of comfort and safety, but even a small disturbance in our life bursts this bubble and we are then forced to see what we had left unexplored until now. I was the same. But now, just one empty memory slot had brought me on this road trip toward this mine. I guess this is what makes life so special. It never fails to surprise us.

After a short ride, I reached the entrance to the mine. The area seemed deserted. The only thing stopping me from entering the mine was an old and tattered wooden sign that read "closed". I did a quick scan of the entrance for any life or heat signatures, but couldn't find any. I pulled up the GPS and tried to pinpoint the location with the help of the previous coordinates. It looked as if the location was somewhere in the center of the mine.

I switched to night vision mode and headed for the location. Honestly, being a droid at this time was coming in handy. There was an old rail track that ran through the mine. I kept on it. I was now able to guess the location and have a virtual map guide me through the mine. It took me around thirty minutes to reach halfway to the location. But to my surprise, it was a dead end.

"What? Seriously?" I thought.

I looked around to see if I could find anything that made sense. For quite some time I just stood there, dumbfounded. What was the meaning of all this? I couldn't just wrap my head around it. "Ah, well fuck it!! Some son of a bitch tricked me I guess." I muttered and turned to go back. But as soon as I turned, I was facing a wall.

What!!? What the F.... I quickly glanced at my map. It was still showing that I was in the same place as before. But it doesn't make any sense. How is this even possible?

I tried to touch the wall in front of me. It felt kind of fluffy. "Strange... Isn't it?" I thought. I don't remember walls being made of foam. I tried to push through it. And to my surprise, it just popped open.

WHAT!!!

But I noticed something. As the wall popped open and disappeared, it sent a wave of green lines through each of the walls. It looked mesmerizing as the lines scanned all the walls and left a darker shade of black on them. And now it all made sense to me.

The mine was a large-scale hologram. It was not REAL! HOLY SHIT!!!

I turned around, and according to the virtual map, I was facing in the direction of the location. I braced myself and ran toward the location. I was a little skeptic, but I ran into the wall. And Puff! It vanished. There was another wall in front of me. I ran through it. Puff! Same result.

I was getting confident and excited now. I quickly increased my speed.

PUFF! PUFF!! PUFF! The walls were vanishing.

I couldn't even remember how many walls I had come through. I was just going with the flow.

I was getting closer to the location. From what I could figure out, only one more wall was left now. So I ran toward it.

And then…
BANG!!!
"ERROR: Critical damage received. Entering recovery mode" was all I saw. And then everything went dark.

THE LAB

"Recovery complete... Initializing systems….." flashed in complete darkness.

I was slowly able to open my eyes. It took me a minute to get up and regain senses of my surroundings. As I looked around, it dawned on me that I had gone on full force into an actual steel wall.

"Stupid!!" I said to myself.

I got up and dusted my clothes. The wall I had crashed into had a light strip at its top running on its entire length. I could now see that the wall ended in a rock in the left and then stretched to the right. I decided to follow it.

After some time, I came across a steel door. At first glance, it looked like it could only be opened from the inside, as there were no knobs or handles visible. I started to touch and feel the door to find any cracks or any pop-up knobs. After running my hand slowly around the door, I was able to feel a very slight slit in the door. The slit started from the top right side of the door and then came down and ended a few centimeters wide in the shape of a rhomboid at the right side center of the door. I pressed on it and then heard a click.

I moved away from the door. The rhomboid rotated inside out and revealed a small keypad with a small analog display which displayed "ENTER CODE".

"Hmm, well that's a very sophisticated security system for such a facility." I thought while smirking.

I started punching in random number combinations as I had no clue what the code was.

0000- ACCESS DENIED

1111- ACCESS DENIED

1234- ACCESS DENIED

4321- ACCESS DENIED

1357- ACCESS DENIED…

After about a hundred failed attempts, I got bored and stopped. I then decided to just close my eyes and think of a random combination.

So, I closed my eyes and started thinking. The combination that popped up was 6539. I entered it.

6539- ACCESS GRANTED

"Seriously! You've got to be kidding me. This has to be some kind of joke." I thought. The door slid open. There was a stairway leading downwards. "Okay, fuck it! Let's just see this thing through." I grunted as I proceeded into the stairway.

On reaching the bottom of the stairs, I was standing at the entrance of a huge lab. It extended into every direction as far as the eyes could see. I could see huge glass cylinders, which almost touched the ceiling, lined up until the end. The cylinders had some sort of liquid inside. They all looked very beautiful in different shades of purple, green, and blood red. The liquids were swirling and it looked as if the cylinders were some kind of mixing tanks. I couldn't see anyone in the lab. I assumed that this was some sort of autonomous facility. I decided to take a look around.

As I walked in between the rows of the glass cylinders, I was able to see that the cylinders were all connected and had valves preventing their liquids from mixing. The cylinders had one central pipe that linked all of them. Its end was inside a huge cylinder almost thrice the size of the other cylinders. This cylinder was empty and it looked like the other cylinders sent their fluids inside this one for final mixing.

As I was walking by, I remembered something. I decided to open my GPS and look for the coordinates. It looked like the location was in the far-right direction, so I went for it. On my way to the location, I came across some cylinders that contained some sort of translucent and yet luminescent liquid. It was glowing with a faint green light. I was not sure what it was so I just went past them.

On reaching my destination, I just stood, mesmerized with what was in front of me. It looked as if somebody had reached out and torn the fabric of space. What I saw was a glowing purple circle hanging in mid-air. It had no other side and was completely non-existent once you went around it. It looked like a door to some other world. The purple circle had a boundary, but the center looked like a vortex of swirling purple and white light. The circle was in between two huge mechanical circular claws which looked as if they were trying to stop it from opening wider.

CLICK! SHOOK! CLICK!

I immediately turned around to see a middle-aged white man. His face was bright red, and his stance seemed a bit flimsy to me. He was sweating all over and was wearing a white lab coat over his clothes. His eyes flinched as he aimed his rifle at me.

"Don't you fucking try to move! Asshole!" he screamed.

"Hey! Woah! Calm down man!" I said nervously while raising my hands in the air.

"See man, no weapons! I am not here to harm you, man! Chill!" I added.

"Harm me?" he chuckled. "I am gonna fucking pop your head before you even flinch. Now lie on the ground and put your hands where I can see them!"

I obeyed.

He walked toward me to do a cursory search.

"Okay, stand up with your hands behind your head. And walk into the scanner." he said, pointing to the body scanner placed nearby.

The body scanner is kind of a large glass case mounted with different sensors. They are used to detect bombs and other metal objects. But the scanner he was referring to looked a bit different in the context that it had way too many sensors attached to it as compared to the normal scanners I had seen at airports.

I walked into it and the door closed.

He hurriedly walked up to the control console and started pressing some buttons. The sensors seemed to have come to life and my entire body was being scanned by a stream of green and blue lasers.

I didn't want to surprise him by the results, so I said, "Hey man...Ah... sir... Just letting you know that I am a droid."

"A droid?" he said.

"Yup, I am. I wasn't before, but technically speaking, I am a virtual orphan. And just saying, you had no reason to search me if you already had a scanner." I replied.

"But how did you get in...Ah.. you are a droid.. then how did you...?" he started to question himself and went into some deep thoughts.

I did not know how to respond, so I just kept quiet while the scanner did its job.

After a few minutes of awkward silence, the machine stopped and I could see the control console read "Processing Data..."

"By the way, my name is Max." I said from my glass cage.

"Oh, yeah... yeah. I am Alfred... Alfred Grey," he replied absent-mindedly, still engrossed in his thoughts.

"You are Alfred grey? The Alfred Grey... The inventor of the AMD's... Alfred Grey?" I asked.

"Yeah... Yeah... the same," he replied in the same absent-minded tone while still looking into the console.

"What? This... This... is not possible!!" he suddenly exclaimed.

"What? What happened?" I asked.

"You said you were a droid, right?" he asked.

"Yes," I replied

"Who is the manufacturer?" he asked.

"Corning industries," I said.

"Serial number?" he enquired.

"Ah... HX12B-BX56C-V101," I replied.

"Okay, wait, let me check." he said and started typing my serial number in the control console.

"Hmm. Interesting... this does check out," he said.

"Okay... So you are not here to steal from me, right?"

"Yes... I have been trying to explain to you the same since I got here." I said.

"Oh, okay...I'll let you out. But I have some questions for you." he said. He seemed to have calmed down a bit.

I nodded.

He opened the scanner's door and put two stools in front of the console. He sat on one of them and signaled me to sit on the other.

As I settled down, he said " Hi, I am Alfred. Sorry for the behavior earlier. I just had to be sure about you."

"Oh, okay, no issues. It's fine." I replied.

"So, son, I have few questions for you." he said.

"Oh, okay, but I too want to ask you something." I said.

"Okay. But first, let me complete. Tell me how you got here."

"Ahh... It's a long story, but in short, I got a hologram message which brought me to the location of that." I said, pointing at the portal.

"Hmmm. Okay... but how did you get in here?" he asked.

"Through the door. You have a keypad lock for this place. I just punched some numbers and I was able to get inside." I said.

"See, first let me tell you something about the keypad lock. The keypad lock is a dud. The real scanner is the one mounted on the wall opposite to the door. That is not visible to most. That scanner scans for brainwave activities. Each person has a definite pattern of brain waves, which is linked to their thought process. The scanner matches the brain wave pattern and the door opens only if the pattern is recognized to be of an authorized person."

"Wait a minute. For the brain waves to be generated, I need to have a brain first. I mean to say that I need to be a human first. But I am a droid. I only have the NBLC chip that's inside my head. And as far as I know, the NBLC does not emit any brain waves."

"Yeah, but this is exactly what I wanted to tell you. Look here." he handed me a tablet console.

"You have a brain in your head, an actual human brain that is fused with the chip on a molecular level. And that was the most baffling thing I found. You have a human nervous system within you. This is independent of your mechanical nervous system..." he said.

"What?!!" I exclaimed. "Are you sure about what you are saying?" I added.

"Yeah you can have a look at yourself." he said, pointing to the tablet. I looked at it and it was indeed true.

"But tell me something. If this was the case, why was it not found until now? I have gone to the repair shop numerous times, even recently. The repair guy didn't find anything unusual with me. How do you explain that?" I asked.

"Well... See, it must be a bit difficult to understand. But this scanner that you just went into has far more precision than the commercially available ones. And it seems that there is an inhibitor which masks the brain waves and the actual brain is located in a closure inside your skull. And what the repair guy saw was the mock of NBLC placed above the closure. And that is why no issues were reported." he said.

"Okay, I get that part. But what about the time when my mechanical nervous system was replaced? Had there been any other neuron in my body or anything like that, it should have been reported, right?" I inquired.

"Ah. I think that is because at that time, the neural network was not there. This is just my speculation, but it looks like the human neural network that you have has grown recently."

"Grown..?" I asked quizzically.

"Yeah... it's just a theory though, because the dendrites still seem to be in a growing phase." he said.

"So, what exactly is this place?" I asked. "Is that a portal?" I added.

"This is my lab, the very same place where I invented the model for AMD's. I believe that can be referred to as a portal, but till now, I haven't been able to figure out what it is. It just popped open one day. I have kept it a secret by hiding its energy signature in a containment field. I still have to figure out what lies on the other side." he said.

"Okay, but what if I tell everyone about it?" I said with a smirk.

"See, there is always a remote kill button installed in every AMD. I will just make use of that. So you are no threat to me anyway." he said.

I did not know how to respond, so I kept quiet.

"Come, I'll show you something." he said.

I followed him to one small room at the far end of the lab.

This room was well-lit and had some sort of consoles lining up both sides of the room. At the end of the room, there was a humanoid mechanical figure held in place by some metal stands. It looked like a pre-manufacturing test robot on its display stand. It had a titanium shell, like mine. But it was a more refined version of my model. It had more robust-looking arms and legs and its chest was also very wide.

"So, what is it?" I asked.

"It is a prototype that I am working on. You can refer to it as AMD v2.0. Once this is completed, people will not be forced to store their consciousness in the NBLC and can directly have their brain installed along with an NBLC in a new body once their physical body gives up. The reason behind this is that the NBLC method is still not 100% efficient and there have been times the consciousness itself gets corrupted while being transferred. Corning does not want anyone to know about it, so such cases are quickly silenced. But it seems to me now that somebody beat me to it." he said.

"How?" I asked.

"Because you are the living and functioning model of this prototype." he said.

"No... But... I am from corning industries." I spoke nervously.

"That is what baffles me. The technology needed to develop it is still being developed. Hell! I am the one working on it. Then how…" he paused. "I need to know more about you." he added.

[RADIATION LEVELS RISING! CONTAINMENT FIELD REACHING MAXIMUM CAPACITY!]

A computer voice announced and the entire lab went red. All alarms went off.

Before I could figure out what was happening, Alfred bolted out of the room. I hurriedly followed him. He ran toward the portal's control console and started to hurriedly type something. In the meantime, I saw the portal's light vortex growing rapidly, as if it was going to burst out. It was clear that the containment field was not holding up. Now I could see the previously invisible containment field trying to keep up with the portal spewing out yellow light, just like a balloon filled with water bulges as we start to force all the water in one direction. Then it seemed that a small sliver of yellow light managed to move through the field. And within a fraction of a second, I was facing a yellow stream of light which was about to hit me. I tried to turn and run. But it was too late. As the light hit me, I was surrounded by a yellow hue. And after that, it was total darkness.

The Portal

[Initializing Systems…]

As my eyes came into focus, I realized that I was on a metal bench. I looked around to see Alfred dozing off on a stool next to my bench. I tried to get up, but it looked like I was unable to move my hands or feet. My head felt heavier and my eyes started to drop again. I was in complete darkness once again.

"Hey, wake up. You okay?" I heard a voice.

I opened my eyes to see Alfred looking at me.

"Yeah, I am okay. What happened?" I asked while trying to sit up.

"Well, you were hit by the energy from the portal, which knocked you out. Either way, no serious damage was done." he said.

"Knocked out? For how long?"

"Eh... Not much. Just a couple of days."

"Days?!!"

"Yeah. Don't worry, I returned your rented bike to the town. I found about it when I cross-checked the video log of the day you came. Now get up and follow me. I have to show you something." he said.

I was now feeling like myself again.

"Wait, you have security cameras in place? Then how did you not see me coming?" I asked.

"Because for some reason, the system thinks of you as an authorized person." he said.

"But isn't this your lab? Who else is authorized to enter here?" I asked.

"Yes, that's exactly what I wanted to show you here. Take this and tell me what you see." he said, handing me a tablet computer.

The tablet had three graphs with waveforms like sine waves. One was orange, one was yellow, and one was blue. The orange graph had alternate peaks and troughs, the yellow graph had two steep peaks in the middle, and the blue had alternate peaks and troughs.

"What is this?" I asked.

"This is the data of brainwaves. The orange and yellow ones are yours, but the blue one is mine. The orange and blue look alike." he said.

"Yeah, so?" I said.

"I mean, how do you explain that the brainwaves of two people are exactly in sync? Unless and until…"

"One is mimicking the other," we both said in unison.

"What? That's ridiculous!! How is that even possible, and how do I have two brain waves and you have only one? This doesn't make any sense." I said

"I never said it did. I just said what it means. And the other yellow graph you see only came up after you were hit by the light, As if it activated a dormant state of your brain or something. I think that is why my security system was not triggered as it mistook you for me." he said.

"And yeah, from my observations until now, the energy from the portal destroys any matter that it comes in contact with. But in your case, it boosted your brain activity. Maybe you are compatible with the energy that the portal emits. So, you might find the answers you seek in there." he said while pointing to the portal.

"I have a memory log that I cannot access. Can you first take a look at that?"

"Okay. Let me see." He hooked me to the tablet. "I can see the directory you are talking about"

"Okay, can you access it?"

"Yes, I can. But it won't be of any use."

"Why?"

"Because it's an empty directory."

"What?"

"Yeah, you were not able to access it because your system was trying to read from an empty directory."

"Yes I saw that too. But I thought I was mistaken at first and the files would reappear once my system re-calibrated itself."

"Your memory sector must have been corrupted, but when you tried to access it again and again in the process of recovering the log, the contents got deleted and discarded as junk data."

"Oh…" I said with a sigh.

"Enter the portal Max."

"What did you just say?" I asked.

"Nothing." He replied.

"No, I just heard it. You told me to enter the portal."

"Why in the world would I say that? I am right beside you."

"But..."

"Okay, never mind."

"Come home Max," I heard a voice again.

"What the Fu...?"

I frantically looked around to find the source of the sound, but I couldn't.

"Oh, fuck it! I want to go through the portal."

"Are you sure?" he asked.

"Yes."

"Okay, I'll prepare for your journey then."

"Okay, fine."

There had been so much commotion in my life by now that I had become tired of it. So, even entering an unknown portal seemed like a viable solution if it led me to any answers.

A New World

As I stood in front of the portal, all I could see was a sea of purple lights. But now they had a tinge of warm glow in them.

So I took my first step. It felt like stepping on a large and hard piece of jelly. As I slowly pushed through it, I was able to keep my foot on something solid. I pressed on it and moved through the portal. It was easier than expected. I just slid through it.

When I was completely through, my vision cleared and I was able to see my surroundings. I realized that I was in some sort of forest that had been burned down. As far as I could see, I was only able to see burned trees and the ground was covered in ash. The sky was clear, but it seemed that it was going to be dark soon as I could see the dying sunlight in the distance.

"Well, not such a welcoming place, is it?" I thought.

"Welcome home Max." I heard the voice again. And before I could react, I realized that the portal had vanished into thin air.

"Who are you?" I asked.

"Follow the sun," the voice said.

"What?"

I waited for a reply, but none came.

So I started to walk in the direction of the sun. After walking for some time, I could see an old building. It looked abandoned as there were no lights and half of the roof seemed to have collapsed.

As I reached the entrance of the building, I could see more clearly that the building was at least eight to ten stories high and also had a fence wall, which had now fallen under natural forces. The fence wall seemed to circle around the building and meet at the main gate. The main gate was a sliding one. I slid it open and walked through it. I was standing in a circular corridor that ran in both breadth and height as the building, the ground floor was very spacious and the floors looked neatly stacked like discs in a tray. The inside of the building resembled a closed human rib cage.

"Go to your right and take the stairs to the basement." I heard the voice again.

I obeyed.

As I went down, the stairs ended in front of a huge steel door. I tried to open it, but it didn't budge.

"Look to the right." The voice said.

I looked and found a dust-covered keypad. As I cleared the dust, I could see a number keypad with an LED screen. I wasn't sure if it was in working condition, so I pressed a few buttons to check.

Nothing happened.

As I started looking for an ON switch. I suddenly heard a faint voice from the console.

"Hello, this is JADE. Please enter the code to proceed."

"JADE… So you are JADE…" I smirked and then entered the code.

225-456-998-764-598

Code accepted. I heard the voice confirming.

And then the doors opened.

The doors were an entrance to another stairwell that went downwards. I took them. On reaching the end, the lights turned on automatically. It was a huge lab of some sort, but the more I saw, the more I got confused. Because what I was looking at looked like a mirror image of Alfred Grey's lab.

The lab was dusty, but looked intact. As I walked into the lab, I could figure out that it was empty. But from memory, as I walked further, I reached the place where the portal was in Alfred's Lab. There was a huge screen with a few chairs in front of it. There was also a huge console that spanned the breadth of the screen.

My curiosity was so piqued at this time that I immediately started to push the buttons. I knew it was stupid. But again, what else was there to do. So, I don't know which button triggered the screen, but all of a sudden, the screen lit up. A video came up, in which a middle-aged man, around the age of forty, with black hair, wheatish skin, and really sharp eyes was in a lab coat,   frantically pacing from left to right in front of the camera. He looked stressed about something and was muttering to himself. Then suddenly, he looked into the camera, as if he was able to look at me and said "Okay, let's get this shit done, please get a chair first…" he didn't have a rough voice. It was a very composed and well-paced voice. Like he knew what he was talking about.

I obeyed.

He continued.

"So, this will be a recording with very limited interactive features by the time you see it. Don't worry, Jade will be able to help with some of your questions, but I'll try to explain as much as I can. My name is Maxwell Blake. I am the lead scientist of the government-led research for harnessing dark matter from space to be used as fuel. But in this research, we uncovered, or rather, found something that we shouldn't have. When our rockets were launched to extract a large chunk of dark matter that was just outside our solar system-

Oh, first, let me tell you something about us so that these things will make more sense to you. We are known as Klarkens. I know you come from a world of humans. Our species are twins, who live worlds apart. We believe that we have lived a little longer than humans according to the advancements that we have had in terms of technology and culture. Your language English is primitive. It is a subset of our language Pestonia. I will keep using English to make it more understandable to you.

But yeah, now about our rockets… When they entered the dark matter cloud and started to extract it, one of the rockets found an entire planet hidden inside this cloud. So we had to change our plans and explore this planet. From this planet, we found a rock which we call lycite. Now, lycite was beyond anything we had found before. Even with our technological advancement, we had no clue as to what it was. But once we purified it, this piece of rock was able to bend space and time around it. Upon further research, we found that it had this strange property to completely change its form and become any other element if it was left alongside it for some time. Be it gold, uranium, calcium, neon, water, anything. Be it solid, liquid, or gas, lycite was able to just become it. Even cells, be it human, animal, or plant cells, lycite was able to transform into them.

So, one of the teams that was working on Lycite had also formulated that it could hypothetically open a portal to other dimensions. And one of their scientists was even trying to prove it. He had some interesting results to show us, but just one day after our discussions with them, their entire facility was burned down to the ground, including the people. The island where their facility was located was charred black. The locals from nearby islands only said that they heard a loud HMMM… sound and a blue light came from the sky, after which the entire island was gone in an instant. Strangely, the light was undetected by our planetary defense systems. So, all the research teams were distributed around our world to work in secret. But any time any research team found or was on the verge of finding something about lycite, they would just vanish. Locals reported the same loud HMM sound and the same blue light from the sky every time.

I know it will be a lot to take in, but hear me out. The human body has different cells. There are nerve cells that make up the nervous system, blood cells which make up the blood, skin cells that make up the skin, and so on. Each of these cells has a specific purpose and a definite lifespan. But there is one cell known as the stem cell. There are various types of stem cells, but what makes them stand out is that stem cells can transform into any other cell.

Lycite was unchartered territory for us. We did not know what we were dealing with. But one thing we knew for sure was that we were dealing with something much superior to us.

The stem cell concept has always been intriguing to me. And since people had started to abandon lycite in fear of the blue light, I decided to take matters into my hand. I attempted to link my brain with one sample of lycite. That's when it hit me, that lycite was not a substance or a thing or even matter for that purpose, but rather a stem cell for our universe, the basis for everything. And the reason it was so easily able to morph into an entirely different object was that lycite was only raw code, meaning none of us is real. We all are code, and lycite was only copying the pattern of each object in our world to become it.

As I realized it, I didn't know what to do or how to react. When I fused my brain with lycite, I was able to see your world as well and I also gained the knowledge of how to reach out into your world.

You know, the biggest flaw in any sentient species is that it considers itself to be the topmost in the food chain. So it always tries to find a way to justify its existence within the boundaries of its thinking and rejects any idea that challenges or is beyond its level of understanding. Take an example of the evolution of your species. You believe that you descended from apes. Why? Because you connected the dots about finding things buried in your ground and doing DNA analysis on them. Your ego was satisfied as you proved your superiority in finding your ancestors. But not once did you question if it was possible that you were made to think that you were descendants of apes and not an upgraded version of them.

The reason I say this is because, in my link, this is what I realized, that your world and mine and many others were not worlds at all, just programs or simulations running on God knows what and by God knows who. And these portals and space-time bridges are just backdoors into these programs. And now, do you know the best way to describe the multiverse? Nothing mumbo jumbo or any fancy sci-fi shit. It's just parallel processing of different programs, that's all. Space, time, and the limit of travelling at the speed of light are just parameters and constraints to keep us in check. That is why, even though we understand and acknowledge the possibility of time travel, we still spend our entire lives moving in linear time, in just one direction. Because that's what we have been programmed to do. I do have a term coined for our lords. I call them the programmers. I know it's not fancy, but it does give us some perspective.

Now, the reason why I brought you here.

Yeah, don't look so surprised. You didn't think everything that has happened until now was just a coincidence, did you?"

"Oh, no... No. Not at all."

"Yeah, good. Because if you did think it, you are only an idiot. That's all. HEHE." He smirked. "I know that by now you must have an identity of your own and would have become a different person. But the truth is that you are my son."

"What?" I said.

"Yes, I knew that finding so much about lycite was going to be a deadly trade. And if you are seeing this, then you know what I am talking about. I knew the programmers will come after my entire species for this, and there was nothing I could do to stop them. So, I decided to give this knowledge to you, my son. So that you can save other worlds from going through the fate that my world has gone through. Because eventually, someone in some other world will somehow find anything that they should not and it will eventually lead to their annihilation.

So, your mom and my colleague Samantha came up with the idea of passing this information to you, but when you were an infant, the attacks began. So we had to evacuate and come to this place.

I wanted to give you all my memories too, to keep you from looking for clues in the dark. But we didn't have enough time. So I had to implant a basic version of commands in your brain. These are the voices that you keep hearing. Your brain was designed to look like a normal human brain, but it could emit frequent brain waves that could affect the person in front of you and he or she will perceive you as a normal being even if they find anything abnormal about you. I did this only so that you can grow up and be able to come back here. I just wish I'd have given you more. Your mother and I will always love you, just remember that…

And the video ended.

Just then, it hit me. The dream I had previously about a man and a woman in the forest, was not a dream, but a memory from my father's last day in this world. And the woman was my mother.

Now I knew what I had to do.
"Jade," I said.

The computer screen lit up and I could see a female face smiling at me, "Yes, how can I help you?" she said.

"I want to learn everything that my father and his people have worked upon." I said.

"Okay, sure. Please head to the virtual library section on the east side of this facility." she replied.

"Yes, sure."

TEN YEARS

Ten years later.

I could hear the birds chirping. I climbed to the top of the facility. I did not wish to miss the sunrise. As far as I could see, there was a mix of green and dark patches. The forest appeared to be healing. As the golden rays of the sun hit the crest of the trees, it looked like I was looking at a sea of gold. The aura was just mesmerizing.

Ten years have passed since I came to this place. Even with my enhanced capabilities as a droid, it took me ten years to fully learn and understand what my dad's species had achieved in their time. Even though lycite was my main focus, the advancements in science, technology, and medicine that these people had made are astonishing. And it took me a lot of time to learn their tricks of the trade when it came to communication. In my world, we have only heard of telepathy, but these people were masters of it. Even children here were able to do it.

In these ten years, I also tried to find pieces for my origin as well. I was able to finally remember what happened that night. It turned out that my dreams were my father's memories, and the capsule in the dream was the orb that brought me to Alfred's lab. My dad had opened a portal to Alfred's lab and sent an infant me through that portal. The capsule had a link to my dad. Just before he died, he used Lycite to morph space and time to send the capsule behind the infant me. The capsule was always linked to me as my dad had programmed it, but it hibernated after entering my world. And from what I deduced, when the blue light hit me, my brain waves got boosted, which in turn activated the capsule to find me as it did in the bus.

At first, what baffled me was, how did I turn into a virtual orphan? Later I discovered that it was just a simple trick. My dad had telepathically programmed my brainwaves to affect the people near me. So, when I was diagnosed with bone marrow cancer, during the transfer of my consciousness into the NBLC chip, my brain waves tricked the engineer or whosoever was doing it into building a safety hatch for my brain to rest in. It also happened when the engineer opened me for repair. And this brings us to Alfred's lab. The reason I was able to enter through the security was not that my brainwaves mimicked Alfred's brain waves. Instead, they hacked into the system as Alfred. Even after all this time, one thing never became clear to me. Why did dad wait till the last minute to send me the capsule and not simply transfer it while he sent me?

All the time that I had spent here made me realize one thing though. These programmers keep watch on all of us. I still don't understand how frequently or how they do it, but one thing is for sure. They do keep watch and if anything defies their will, it just gets annihilated.

This world was in shambles, for as far as I could venture, I found out that the Klarkens were specifically chosen and terminated. My father said that I had to protect my world. At first, I didn't see any sense in it. Why should I put myself in harm's way to protect other beings when my world was already destroyed? And secondly, the world of humans was literally in another plane of existence. So it made no sense to me. But those asshole programmers took my parents away from me. Savior or not, I had a bone to pick with those motherfuckers, and I was going to do it, no matter the cost.

Oh yeah, now I would like to tell you some cool things that I learned in these ten years. You see, the klarkens had also discovered this metal known as Linos. In an unpurified state, linos was ten times stronger than titanium and had ten times higher melting point than tungsten from the human world. So I slowly and gradually replaced my body parts with this metal. Nanotech seemed very common in this world, so I also have thrusters built into my body now. I am still a novice at flying and taking off like any superhero, but it's a work in progress.

The portal I came through closed once I entered this world. And with the help of my father's research, I was able to build a portal device. I decided to go back to the human world because this world didn't have any intelligent species left, so I figured this world was not of much interest to the programmers now. And I also figured that if the humans are still alive, then the programmers must have kept a watch on them and once I figure out how they are keeping watch, I'll be able to go and face them myself.

THE
PROGRAMMERS

Travelling back to the human world was risky. But it was a risk that I had to take. The device I was able to make was a gravity bender. It would generate a force field around it, and rapidly generate so many gravitational waves that it would split the space-time plane so that I can enter the other world. It was powered by lycite. The force field around it would prevent it from collapsing onto itself and creating a black hole. I figured out when I was in my father's world that lycite or some other equivalent should be available in my world as well, so my device would try to pinpoint the energy signature of lycite or its closest resembling waveform and open a portal to the place where the energy signature was strongest.

So, with a deep breath, I started the device. I could see that at first, the device got covered in a golden sphere, which then started to expand. In a few seconds, there was a circular door-like opening levitating a few centimeters above the ground. The inside of the opening glowed with a dreamy blue hue. I walked right into it. It felt like walking through a tunnel made out of foam.

As I reached the other side, I could see a black sky with a lot of stars and a narrow pathway leading to what looked like a small village. As I entered the village, there was this eerie silence. At first, I thought that it might be because the people might have slept by now. But still, something didn't feel right. As I walked further, I soon reached a small village square. Now I could guess the layout of the village. The village had a well in the square and the path I took was the entrance which went through the square and then formed a closed half-ring after the square, the center of which was a huge building. At first, it looked like the village church. Houses lined both sides of the path.

I decided to enter the church. As I entered the church, I could see a dimly-lit altar and a row of seats on both sides of the aisle. A person was sitting on the far left on the first row of the aisle.

As I approached him, I could see that he was the priest.

"Hello, Father,"

"Hello…" he greeted me.

"Have I arrived too late in the night?" I said.

"No son, more people used to gather here and this place used to be very lively. But the gods didn't see it fit I guess." he replied.

"I don't understand." I said.

"You see, this is a miner's village and everything was good until a few months ago. They mined a new kind of rock and brought it to the village. The village chief was very happy and wanted to sell it to gain more profits. The village people also agreed. But the night when everybody was enjoying and celebrating, a loud sound was heard in the sky and then a blue dash of light fell upon the villagers. Everyone tried to run away, but all the miners who had found the rock vanished instantly. Many families were destroyed that night and since that day, the village has remained quiet. People have started to believe that it was a devil's rock and the gods were angered because of it and that's why they received this punishment. But son, what brings you here?"

"Father, you can say that God has led me to this place. Can I see the rock?" I asked.

"Oh, okay. God works in mysterious ways, son. The rock has since been locked inside a box and is kept inside the church's basement, away from the people. Honestly, I didn't sense any unholy aura from it, and I didn't find anything about this rock in the scriptures either. If you can find anything, then let me know as well. Follow me, I'll show you." He said and led me to the basement.

As he opened the chained box, I could see a huge rock crystal in front of me. This crystal had patches of light green glass all over it, and these patches were pulsating with a faint green light like a heartbeat. To an untrained eye, this would seem like a gem. As I reached out and broke a piece of this rock and held it, this piece didn't have the same weight as it appeared at first and was surprisingly lighter.

Ting! Ting! Ting! I could hear a faint noise and some vibration coming from my back pocket. As I reached out in my pocket, I found out that I had kept a small piece of lycite in a small glass tube and the rock was now trying to get out, as if it was attracted to something. As I brought it closer to the rock in my hand, the lycite piece started to be strongly attracted to it. My suspicions were correct. This was some form of lycite equivalent of this world.

"Father, can I have this piece?" I asked.

"Oh yes, you can. But you have to take it away." he said.

"Okay, I understand." I replied. I knew why he wanted me to leave and it made sense as well.

So I took this small piece and headed outside the village.

Dawn was here and the sky had now become a darker shade of blue. In the morning light, I could see a small hill behind the village.

Now I had an idea, so I started walking toward the hill. As I reached the top of the hill, it became flat and I could see the greenery that surrounded the place.

So I held the rock in my hands on top of my head and screamed on top of my voice.

"HEY! I KNOW WHO YOU ARE. I NEED TO SPEAK WITH YOU. IF YOU DON'T ANSWER ME, I'LL TELL EVERYONE ABOUT LYCITE. YOU HEAR ME. I WILL TELL EVERYONE ABOUT WHO YOU ARE."

And this was followed by utter silence. For a few minutes, I just stood there like a statue, with my hands over my head, holding the rock, waiting for something to happen. But nothing happened. I started feeling like an idiot.

"At least I tried..." I consoled myself and started to walk away.

But suddenly, it got dark and the winds started to blow hard. As I looked up, I could see a cyclone forming right on top of my head.

And then a deafening HMM!! like the previous one I had heard, echoed. And then I could see a blue beam of light coming toward me.

"Oh Fuc…" was all I could manage to say, and then everything quickly became dark.

The Beginning

As I came to my senses, I realized I was sitting on a metal chair inside a huge cylindrical glass chamber. The top of the chamber had a bright white light source, which only illuminated the area inside the chamber and everything around me was covered in darkness. I tried to adjust my eyes to get some view of the place I was in, but it just looked like I was trying to look into a cloud of darkness, so I was unable to figure out where I was.

"Oh, so you are finally awake. I'll inform them." a voice came from behind me.

I turned around, but couldn't see who it was.

A few moments later, I could see three glowing crystals floating toward me. They came and surrounded the glass cage. It was a strange feeling. I could sense their presence, but I was unable to figure out what their body structure was. It was strange. It just felt like I was facing three huge people, but all I could see were three floating crystals.

As I sat there, the crystal floating in front of me lit up. And a heavy yet gentle voice spoke, "Hello Maxwell, how are you?"

"Ah, I am okay. But who are you? And why am I in a cage?"
I asked.

"That's not a cage. It looks like glass, but it is a type of
containment field that is giving your consciousness a bodily form
so that we can talk to you."

"Wait!! What?? Am I dead or something?"

"No, no, don't worry. You are not dead. You can just say
that at present, you are above the plane you exist on."

"But... But why am I here? And who are you?"

"Don't you know us? You came looking for us, didn't you?"

"You are the programmers?"

"Oh, is that what you call us? Not a very fancy name..." he
slightly chuckled.

"So, who are you?" I asked.

"Why does it matter to you?"

"I just want to know who my creator is." I said.

"You can see us right in front of you. And you are
communicating with us right now. This should give you some idea
of who we are."

"Why am I here then? If you don't wish to show your true
self and you are my creator as you say, then you shouldn't need
me, right?

"No, actually we don't. We just found you interesting as
you emerged as an anomaly in our code. That is why we
wanted to speak with you and see if you can help us with
something."

"Your code? But I am a living being, right?" I asked
quizzically.

"Oh, yes, apologies, it must be a new concept for you. You are what we call a piece of organic code, a self-evolving organic code that takes a material form and develops a consciousness. This code resides inside our environment, which you call space. Your entire species and all the things that you see in your world are just one form that the code takes once it's deployed in space. That is why everything is linked in your world, and things seem to have a relationship of action and reaction."

"Hmm, okay. If you say that the code is self-evolving, then it means that the basic structure of the code is the same, right?"

"Yes, true."

"Then tell me, why do disease, death, poverty, and pain exist in the world? Why can't everyone have what they want and live the way they want to?"

"See, diseases are a result of the organic code going corrupt and infecting other codes and death is a way of recycling the code. But don't put the blame of poverty on us. We didn't create money. It was the invention of your species. We gave your entire species a fair chance. For this, we made time universal and bound you to move only in linear time, and if we talk from your planet's perspective, everyone has twenty-four hours in a day. Money is your undoing."

"So, why go through all this hassle? What is the point of all this?" I asked.

"See child, we are experimenting on civilization. And trying to chart a way so that an evolving species like yours doesn't annihilate themselves once they attain enough awareness and technological advancement. Till now, we've had thirty-two failed attempts. You and your world are the thirty-third version.

And if I take an example from your world, this is just like the thing you do your in your world, I believe it's called cooking. The recipe is always the same, but the way the food is cooked changes the taste of the dish entirely. And so we need your help in helping us so that this dish does not burn again."

"Oh, really? And what makes you think I will help you after your blue beam killed my parents?"

"You know, if you disobey us, we can still wipe you instantly."

"Oh yes, I do, I surely do. But you won't do it".

"And what makes you say that?"

"Because if you wanted to do it, we would not be having this conversation right now, would we?"

"HAHAHAHA, like father like son. Interesting, very interesting. I do like you Maxwell, you know," he laughed.

"Your father was among the first to figure out who we were. We first thought that silencing him would just end anomalies in the program. But he still outsmarted us, even during his last minutes. He does have our respect for that. And who said that we killed your parents?"

"What?"

"Yeah, we knew that their code had potential, so when our recycling ray hit them, we collected their code and stored them. They are currently inactive. Yes, and the blue ray is not a death ray, it's a collector and recycle ray. It collects and converts the code to its original state. Now you see, I think there is a way we both can help each other."

"And what is that?"

"Until now, we let the code evolve itself and didn't interfere with its understanding of its world. But this time, we want someone to be a guide to them. And what could be better than another code? We want you to be that guide. If you agree, we promise to have your parents be with you. You only have to succeed in this venture and guide the civilization with your knowledge of right and wrong so that they don't annihilate themselves and continue to live on and prosper. If you succeed in this, you'll have what you have always wished for."

"So, if I don't get this correctly, then the entire history of humans will eventually repeat, right? And if everything will start again, then doesn't it mean that all our current technological advancements like NBLC and the knowledge we have already gained will become pointless? So, what makes you think I'll be able to change that? And you also mean that I must play some sort of God, right?" I asked.

"First of all, your codes are designed in such a way that every new experience or knowledge gets absorbed in your original core and when the next iteration happens, this accelerates the evolution process as a whole. So your knowledge base won't go to waste. Now, if you talk about everything starting from the beginning, then this is what experimentation is all about, Max. We try again and again until the desired result is achieved. And we are not asking you to play God. For this version of the world, we will make you one. So, do we have a deal?"

The image of my parents flashed before my eyes. "Okay, we have a deal." I replied shortly.

"Remember Max, the purpose of humans is only to live and let live. We'll be watching over you. Farewell." he said.

And the light's intensity started to increase so much that I felt that I was going to go blind. And then suddenly, there was complete darkness.

As I tried to open my eyes, I realized I was floating. I tried to wake up, but as soon as I came to my senses, I could see a silver line running along my body. There was darkness all around me, except for the fact that I could see stars all around me. Then I turned around. To my proper realization, I was floating in space at some distance from planet earth. I tried to move toward it and my thrusters kicked in. I was able to smoothly fly toward it and it felt great.

As I gently entered the earth's atmosphere, I could see greenery everywhere. It seemed that the programmers had reset this world, but I was not sure what had happened to all the humans. As I was gliding through this lush green field, I could now see a huge tree in the distance. This tree had something of an odd look. I was not sure how, but I could see the code that generated it running across it. As I went closer, I could see that parts of it had not been completely generated and it had some bad code running through it. As I landed to find out more about it, I started to take a walk around it. On the other side, a man and a woman were lying unconscious on the ground. They looked young and had ragged clothes on.

They must have come in contact with the tree and hurt themselves. So I decided to try to wake them up to make sure they are okay.

"Hey, are you both alright?" I sat beside them and tried to wake them by giving them a nudge.

After a while, the guy woke up and soon, the girl woke up too. Something was off about them. They looked at me like they had never seen a person before.

"Are you both okay?" I asked.

They both nodded.

Guy- "Who am I?"

Girl- "Who am I?"

"Oh, not this shit again…" I muttered

Guy- "Shit!"

Girl- "Shit!"

"Oh no! No! No! You cannot say that! It's a bad word. Don't say it, okay?"

"Okay." both replied.

"What are your names?" I asked.

They just looked at each other and then looked at me with a blank expression.

"Ah... Okay, fine. We will discuss this later." I said.

"I better check this place out to see if any other programs are there or they will get themselves killed with this level of intelligence." I thought.

BOOM!!

"Oh fuck!! Now what the hell is that supposed to mean?" I said.

Guy- "Fuck."

Girl- "Fuck."

"No!!!! You cannot say Fuck. It is also a bad word. Only I am allowed to say that!" I hurriedly replied.

"Listen, both of you. I have to go and check where the noise came from. I'll be right back. Just stay here. For now, let's just call you Adam and Eve. Just don't go near that tree or eat anything from it. It's bad, okay?" I said as I started to lift off.

They nodded in agreement.

And boy was I wrong in trusting those two…